❈ *A Blue-Eyed Daisy*

YEARLING BOOKS are designed especially to entertain and enlighten young people. Charles F. Reasoner, Professor Emeritus of Children's Literature and Reading, New York University, is consultant to this series.

For a complete listing of all Yearling titles, write to Dell Publishing Co., Inc., Promotion Department, P.O. Box 3000, Pine Brook, N.J. 07058.

❋ *A*

Cynthia Rylant

Blue-Eyed Daisy

A YEARLING BOOK

Published by
Dell Publishing Co., Inc.
1 Dag Hammarskjold Plaza
New York, New York 10017

Yearling ® TM 913705, Dell Publishing Co., Inc.

ISBN: 0-440-40927-6

Reprinted by arrangement with Bradbury Press, An Affiliate of Macmillan, Inc.

Printed in the United States of America

January 1987

10 9 8 7 6 5 4 3 2 1

CW

For Gerry

❀ *Fall*

❋ *The Prettiest*

ELLIE'S FATHER WAS A DRINKING MAN. EVERYBODY knew it. Couldn't help knowing it because when Okey Farley was drunk he always jumped in his red and white Chevy truck and made the rocks fly up and down the mountains.

He had been a coal miner. Drank then, too, but just on weekends. A lot of miners drank on the weekend to scare away the coming week.

Okey had been hurt in a slate fall, so he couldn't work anymore. Just stayed home and drank.

Ellie was his youngest daughter, the youngest of five. She didn't look anything like Okey or her mother, both of whom had shiny black hair and dark eyes.

Ellie was fair. Her hair was nearly white and her skin pale like snow cream. Ellie was a pretty girl, but her teeth were getting rotten and she always hid them with her hand when she laughed.

Ellie loved her father, but she was afraid of him. Because when he drank he usually yelled, or cried or hit her mother. At those times Ellie stayed in her room and prayed.

One day Okey did a strange thing. He brought home a beagle. Her father couldn't hunt because his right arm wasn't strong enough to manage a rifle anymore. But there he was with a beagle he called Bullet.

He made Bullet a house. Spent the whole weekend making it and didn't even stop to take a drink.

Then Bullet was tied up to his house, and he kept them all awake three nights in a row with his howling.

Okey would not explain why he'd bought a hunting dog when he couldn't hunt. He just sat on the porch with a bottle in his hand (he'd taken it up again) and looked at Bullet.

Ellie was the only one of Okey's children who took an interest in his pet. The older girls were not impressed by a dog.

But Ellie, fair and quiet, liked the beagle and was interested in her father's liking for it. And when Okey was sober, she'd sit with him on the porch and they'd talk about Bullet.

Neither of them could remember later who mentioned it first, but somehow the subject of hunting came up one day, and, hardly knowing she was saying it, Ellie announced she wanted to learn how to hunt.

Okey laughed long and hard. In fact, he had a little whiskey down his throat and nearly choked to death on it. Ellie slapped his back about fifty times.

The next time they sat together, though, she said it again. And this time more firmly, for she'd given it some thought. And Okey set down his bottle and listened.

He tested her. He set up some cans, showed her how to handle his rifle, then stepped back to watch. The first day she missed them all. The second day she hit one. The fifth day she hit four out of nine.

So when she brought up hunting again, they fixed the date.

They went out on a Saturday about five-thirty in the morning, just as the blackness was turning blue. Ellie was booted and flanneled like her father, and she had her own gun.

Okey held his rifle under his left arm. They both knew he'd never be able to shoot it. But neither said anything.

It was just getting light when they made the top of the mountains, their breaths coming fast and smoky cold. They each found a tree to lean against and the wait began.

Bullet had traveled far away from them. He was after rabbit, they knew that much, and they were after squirrel. Okey told Ellie she might have half a chance of hitting a squirrel. Rabbit was out of the question.

Ellie flexed her fingers and tried not to shiver. She was partly cold and partly scared, but mostly happy. For she was on a mountain with her father and it was dawn.

Neither Okey nor Ellie expected a deer to come along. So neither was prepared when one did. But less than twenty feet away, stamping its front hoof in warning, suddenly stood a doe. Okey and Ellie looked across the trees at each other and froze themselves into the scenery.

The doe did not catch their scent. And she could not see them unless they moved. But she sensed something was odd, for she stamped again. Then moved closer.

Ellie looked at the animal. She knew that if she shot a deer, doe or buck, her father would never stop bragging about it. "First time out and she got a deer." She knew it would be so.

The doe was nearing her tree and she knew if she were quick about it, she could get that deer. She knew it would be easier than shooting a squirrel off a tree limb. She could kill that deer.

But she did not. The doe moved nearer; it was a big one, and its large brown eyes watched for movement. They found it. Ellie raised her arm. And she waved.

The deer snorted hard and turned. It was so quickly gone that Ellie could not be sure in which direction it headed.

"Godamighty!" she heard Okey yell. She knew

7

he might be mad enough to shoot her, if he could hold onto his rifle. She heard his crashing across the ground.

"Now wasn't that," Okey gasped as he reached her tree, "wasn't that the *prettiest* thing you ever seen?"

Ellie hesitated, wondering, and then she grinned wide.

"The *prettiest*," she answered.

And they turned together and went quickly down the mountain to find Bullet and go on home.

❋ *Evening*

ELLIE WISHED FOR ONE THING: A ROOM OF HER OWN.
She had to share a bedroom with her sisters Linda
and Martha, while Eunice and Wanda had another
room for themselves. Ellie had one skinny bed,
one skinny piece of wall for her pictures and two
of the drawers in the bureau.

It was not enough.

She often imagined what it would be like if by
some miracle her four sisters disappeared. She and
Okey would go shopping for wallpaper for her
room. They would walk into the paint and wallpaper store:

"Okay, darlin'. See what catches your eye."
(Okey would call her "darlin'," Ellie figured, if the other girls vanished.)

Ellie imagined hundreds of rolls of wallpaper on display, each with a little piece pulled down from the roll for a good look.

Ellie would walk among them all.

"Daddy, do you think I'm daisies? Or maybe rainbows?"

Okey would shake his head and laugh.

"Just get what you want, darlin'."

Ellie would look slowly and carefully at each of the hundreds of rolls. Which design suited her best? Okey would patiently sit in one of the store's chairs, his legs crossed, and wait.

Then Ellie would find the right paper. She'd pick up the roll and head toward Okey, smiling:

And in the evening, she would fall asleep in her own bedroom, surrounded by a wall full of owls—barn owls, snowy owls, mother owls, baby owls—and beneath the ruffled canopy of her big bed, she would dream.

This is what Ellie thought about as she lay awake in her skinny bed each night, surrounded by sisters who sneezed, grunted, ground their teeth and snored. To have her own room.

She would have liked a little lamp, too. There was just one overhead light in the bedroom, since Okey had said they couldn't afford to put a lamp beside "every blame bed" in the house.

The overhead light made Ellie's eyes hurt.

And she would have liked a bedspread with roses. She had seen one in a Sears catalog once. It had roses about the size of her hand all over the spread, and there were little red satin ribbons on the bottom corners.

Ellie wondered what kind of girl she would be if she had these things. She lay in bed at night, beneath her plain blue bedspread covered with lint balls, and hugged her pillow as she thought about it.

Owls on the walls, roses on the canopy bed, a pretty little lamp and Okey calling her "darlin'."

✳ At the Supper Table

AT EXACTLY FIVE O'CLOCK EVERY DAY, ELLIE'S MOTHER had supper on the table. They had exactly forty minutes to eat and twenty minutes to wash the dishes before "The Channel 4 News" came on. Okey never missed the news unless he was in bed recovering from a drinking bout the night before. Even those evenings, he sometimes staggered out to lie on the couch while Dick Strange gave the report and then staggered back into bed when it was over.

When Ellie was small, suppertime had been the best part of being a Farley. That was when Okey was still working. They had supper late then, almost seven, to give him time to come home from the mine and wash up. Ellie's mother would be frying some pork chops at the stove, Eunice would be cutting up potatoes, Martha would be setting the table, Wanda and Linda would be bickering over who washed dishes last and Ellie would be hiding under the kitchen table, beneath the heavy brown cloth, smelling and listening and waiting for Okey.

It was hard on them all when those days ended. Hard in different ways for each of them. But hardest for Ellie. For she just hadn't had the time the other girls had had to know that kind of suppertime before it all stopped. And it seemed just as she had crawled out from under the table to become part of it all, Okey got hurt and the Farley family, the one she had known, was gone.

And so now suppertime was a somber affair. No one *came home* for dinner. They were all already there. No worker to come through the door tired and dirty and hungry. By the time supper was put on the table, the seven of them had been in the house together a good two hours, usually, with little left to say to each other. Or if one of them had thought of something to tell, it was usually forgotten by five o'clock. Having an outsider (Okey, when he was working) at the table had opened them up to talk. But now there was no outsider, and they all felt too much the heaviness of being alike.

And so the talk at the table was of more practical matters. "Pass me some of them beans, Linda," or, "I don't know about that beef Mr. Facemire is raising—this stuff's pretty tough," and such as that.

It seemed also to Ellie that as her sisters grew older, they grew even quieter at suppertime. Ellie wondered if each of them had some large secret spreading out inside her body which had to be held tightly from five o'clock to six. Now that her sisters had all turned into teen-agers, Ellie wondered how much they knew about important things and how much they were unwilling to tell her, only eleven. Eunice, the oldest, and Wanda, the next, sometimes gave each other a look over the mashed potatoes, and Ellie never missed it. It usually followed some remark Okey had made.

So there were the silence and the secrets of four teen-age girls at the supper table.

Ellie's mother had always been quiet. She was a nervous woman with a nervous laugh, and though she had been welcoming with her warm arms when the girls were all small, she had withdrawn those arms more and more as the girls grew. Now Ellie couldn't remember the last time she had been hugged by her mother. And she saw, when she looked at her, a woman with a thin, set mouth and a wall around her. Okey sometimes broke through that wall when he was drunk and gave her a hard knock on the shoulder. But mostly the wall was there and solid.

After Okey got Bullet, though, the supper table changed some. First, there started some talk between Ellie and him about the dog and about the hunting over on this mountain or that ridge. Ellie loved this talk with Okey in spite of the food and her silent sisters. She actually began to look forward to suppertime and during the day thought of things she could bring up with Okey about the dog or hunting.

And Bullet affected the way the meal ended,

too. They all gave the dog table scraps, so when they finished and began scraping the plates over the scrap bowl, there was some talk among them of Bullet's treats:

"Bullet sure better be thankful for this chunk of fat I saved him."

"You think Bullet'll eat these greens?"

"I swear, that dog eats better than most people."

And saying these things, talking, finally, to each other, they all left the table feeling that it had been a good meal—and that there had been a lot of talk among them, after all.

They all watched "The Channel 4 News" together then, and though the program bored Ellie and probably her sisters, it was worth sitting through to hold that warm feeling that had come from filling Bullet's scrap bowl together.

❋ *Winter*

❋ *Uncle Joe*

ELLIE'S UNCLE JOE WAS A TALL YOUNG MAN WITH blond hair and blue eyes. He was the one who told Ellie her parents found her under a big rock in the hog lot.

Ellie thought the world of her Uncle Joe.

When he graduated from Monroe County High School the spring before, Joe had joined the Air Force. He left home, promising Ellie and her sisters he would send them things from far-off countries. After he had been gone a while, he sent them a picture of himself wearing a jacket with a little fur collar and a cap with funny fur earflaps. Ellie got permission to borrow it for a day and she took it to school with her to brag.

Ellie sometimes liked to call Joe her big brother. But never aloud.

It was when she was walking home from the grocery with her sisters one afternoon in July that Ellie had seen both Okey and her mother sitting on the front steps together. And talking. With each other. Okey wasn't drinking and her mother wasn't crying. They were just talking together like normal people and it had made Ellie positive something was really wrong.

"What's wrong?" she yelled at them before she even came in the yard. They just looked back at her and the other girls and waited for them to get to the house.

"Well?" Ellie asked when they'd reached it.

Okey had looked at her with his head cocked to one side. "Well, Miss Smarty, what makes you figure there's something wrong?"

"You just look it, that's all," she had answered.

"Well, fact is," said Okey, gazing directly at her as the other girls climbed on up the steps, "they're shipping your Uncle Joe into a pretty bad place."

"Bad?" echoed Ellie.

20

"Where there's a war going on."

"*War?*"

"Girl, would you stop repeating me? You heard me."

Martha asked if Joe would likely get killed.

"*Killed?*" Ellie had nearly shouted. Everyone looked at her in disgust. She just couldn't talk in sentences.

"You mean, they're shooting at *our* soldiers there? Like a real war?" There. That had made sense.

Okey looked out past Ellie and all of them.

"Hell, I don't know what a real war is," he had answered.

They had to wait a long time for letters from Joe after he went to the war. Sometimes he'd send them a picture. He had grown a beard. And in one picture, he was holding a board on which sat a live (so he said) scorpion.

Ellie would lie awake at night and be afraid for him. She'd beg God not to let him be shot. Or if he had to get shot, then to let the bullet hit his arm or his foot.

At school in the fall she had told her friends about her uncle who'd gone to war.

One boy told her what his father said about the

war. He told her his father said it was stupid. That soldiers were dying for nothing. That it wasn't even a real war. The boy told Ellie that it must mean her uncle was not a real soldier.

Ellie shoved him hard into the wall. And she called him one of Okey's best cuss words. The boy was so surprised he didn't even fight back—just stared at her with his mouth hanging open.

It seemed, after that, the time would never pass quickly enough until Joe came home. Ellie missed him, but more than that, she wanted him to tell her that he had been a real soldier.

And finally, one afternoon in December when they were nearly snowed in, Joe walked in on them all. He had on his blue uniform and his beard was gone. He seemed a foot taller. And to Ellie, he seemed as old as Okey.

In the night he made fudge in the skillet the way he used to and poured it into a buttered plate to cool. They all sat around the kitchen table, talking. Okey would not talk of the war. Joe would not talk of the war. So no one did.

But before she could sleep, Ellie had to ask him. He was sitting alone in the living room, watching the late news after everyone had gone to bed. All the lamps were off and only the television lit the room, making it blink black and white like the set.

Ellie tiptoed to the doorway. Joe sat on the couch, his long legs sprawled in front of him, and listened to the latest report of soldiers dead. The walls blinked and his face, too, went black, white, black, white, as the pictures crossed the television screen.

Ellie watched him. He looked older than Okey. Old as her grandfather. And when news of the war had finished, he wiped a hand across his eyes.

Ellie silently called the boy at school the strongest cuss word she knew, turned back to her room and fell asleep, tears in her eyes for her Uncle Joe and all the real soldiers.

✳ *Ellie's Christmas*

ELLIE AND HER MOTHER AND HER SISTERS ALL WENT to the Church of God every Sunday. Okey just stayed in bed, sleeping off his Saturday night.

At Christmas everybody at the Church of God drew names and gave gifts. No one was to spend more that fifty cents on a gift. But for some families, like Ellie's, an extra fifty cents was hard to come by at Christmas time. Especially when it was fifty cents times five.

Ellie drew the name of a boy who lived at the mouth of Goldy's Hollow. His name was James Meador, and he was the only child of a truck driver and his wife.

Since Ellie was nearly two years older than James, she knew she should be sensible about giving him a present.

She wasn't.

For days Ellie walked around with the paper bearing James's name on it all wadded up and sweaty in her hand.

Ellie looked at socks in the dime store. And handkerchiefs. She looked at baseball mitts. And at gloves.

Almost everything was over fifty cents. She also didn't like any of it.

Ellie lay awake in bed at night and worried about a gift for James. She imagined what she'd give if she had five dollars to spend and could spend it. She would buy him a paint set. James looked like the kind of boy who would appreciate a paint set with real brushes and paint that didn't wash off. And maybe a little easel.

Ellie fell asleep counting the pots of paint.

A week was left until the big Christmas program, with the play, and the passing out of brown paper bags filled with treats, and the exchanging of gifts. And Ellie still dreamed of paints and still had nothing to give James.

Her mother had started to complain. All the other girls had bought something for somebody at church. Why couldn't Ellie just give James a nice pencil set or a box of colored erasers?

Ellie could not bring herself to buy James a pencil set.

And the night before the Saturday program, Ellie went to bed with still no gift to wrap for James. Her mother had given up on her and had bought James a package of No. 2 pencils in mixed colors.

Ellie lay stiff that night and concentrated. She bit her lower lip until the skin was loose, and she thought. Okey snored, Bullet's chain clinked and the family fell fast asleep, but still she pondered. And when everyone was really dead asleep, she thought of it. She climbed out of bed and headed into the kitchen.

The next day when the Farley women went to church, they each had a package. Including Ellie. It was a wide, flat box that looked like it probably held handkerchiefs. When Ellie's mother saw it, not wrapped but at least tied up with yellow yarn, she put the package of pencils in a kitchen drawer.

When the Christmas play put on by the younger

children ended, the Ladies' Circle members gathered near the pulpit and handed out the treat bags
to everyone.

Then, after all the children (and some of the
adults) had taken a good peek inside their bags to
see just what kind of fruit they'd got and what sort
of nuts and how much rock candy . . . then came
time to open the presents that had been placed under the tree.

To ease the confusion, the congregation was
split up into their regular Sunday School classes,
since that was how the names had been drawn in
the first place. Ellie and James were both in the
Young People's group.

It was difficult for Ellie to guess why James
waited until all the rest had opened their presents
before he opened his own. But Ellie, holding her
breath, as well as the small pack of colored erasers
she'd received, noticed that he did wait. And it
seemed that when the yellow yarn finally came off
the box and the lid was lifted, everybody was ready.

James seemed so surprised, at first, by what he
saw, that his face was simply blank. And then,
slowly, it opened into a smile.

First he drew from the box a large reindeer. It

was a deep red and had horns frosted in sparkling white sugar. Its legs were curved, as though it were leaping—or flying—and a green bell was painted around its neck.

Next James lifted out a snowman. A snowman of rainbow colors—pink face, green arms and a green belly with three blue buttons. He was wearing a top hat of the same deep red as the reindeer, and it was laced with the same sparkling sugar.

James held each cookie up for the others to see as he explored the wide box, and when the box was empty, he sat surrounded by fifteen cookies, each painted and shining and bigger than James's own hand.

Everyone looked longingly at the treasures as James carefully nested each back into the box (Ellie's sisters were just flabbergasted), and Ellie blushed as compliments flew her way. She wished Okey had come.

James was not an eloquent boy and his face had spoken plainly enough, but as everyone left the church for home, he caught up with Ellie and split the reindeer cookie with her.

✳ *Crazy Cecile*

ONE OF ELLIE'S UNCLES —HER LEAST FAVORITE, NAMED Trapper—married a western woman while he was living out in Arizona a while, and he brought her with him when he came home to visit so she could see the snow.

Her name was Cecile, and she reminded Ellie of the witch in *Snow White*. The witch who tried to kill the girl who was fairest in the land. The girl with white skin. Like Ellie's. That witch.

Ellie called her Crazy Cecile when nobody was around to hear.

Crazy Cecile would do things no one else dared

do. Unspeakable things. If the beef was tough and stringy at supper, they could all count on Cecile to say, "Toughest, stringiest beef I've ever eaten."

It made Ellie's mother nervous about her cooking.

And all five girls were absolute wrecks about their looks when Cecile was around. She'd tell one her hair could grease a car, or another her pimples would be improved if she washed regularly. The day she commented on how flat Wanda was, the whole household went into dark corners.

Okey was the only one of them that Crazy Cecile didn't pick on. It was a mystery to them all. Okey cussed too much, drank too much, raced his pickup too much, and he was even growing slightly bald.

Crazy Cecile was unconcerned.

They all tolerated her as best they could. The older girls stayed mostly with friends, Ellie's mother spent hours in the kitchen, Okey ignored her and Ellie wasted more time outside with Bullet.

One night, though, Cecile and Trapper had an argument and he went off in Okey's pickup to buy a carton of cigarettes and blow off steam. Then, Cecile could not be avoided.

She sat at the kitchen table and cried. So they all sat with her, even Okey.

She sobbed and rocked and said Trapper would leave her for sure. Her crying was loud, full of strange sounds from her throat, and her nose dripped. Ellie thought she was disgusting.

No one seemed to know what to say to Cecile. The older girls looked embarrassed. Ellie's mother looked perturbed. Okey looked confused. But no one was willing to leave her.

Cecile wailed and said things about Trapper none of them knew—about Trapper losing his job, getting arrested, wrecking their car.

Her face was awful. Puffed-up eyes, scarlet splotches up and down her neck, and a real mess around her nose.

Ellie wanted to throw up.

But softly, Okey rose from his chair, walked over to the sink and pulled a clean dish towel from the drawer. He held it under some hot water, wrung it out, then came back to the table.

Okey bathed Cecile's face. He held the back of her head with one hand and wiped her tears, using the hot cloth, with the other.

It quieted Cecile. It quieted them all, deep inside. Okey didn't say much. Just, "There now," and "All right, Cecile." But the sight of him bathing that woman's face shook them all.

Cecile sobbed a few times more, then stopped altogether. Okey sat down again and lit up a cigarette.

"Well, Cecile," he said, "looks like you and Trapper have got yourselves some trouble."

Cecile nodded and clutched the dish towel.

"Seems to me," Okey said, "Trapper ought to come home. Live around here somewhere, where he's got family."

Cecile started to nod her head, but then her eyes widened.

"Live *here*?" she said. "In these rotten hills?"

She flipped the dish towel onto the table.

"I'd rather *die*."

She pushed back her chair and went into the living room.

Okey and Ellie and Ellie's mother and the four girls all looked at each other.

Okey grinned.

"That woman's crazy," he muttered.

Ellie giggled.

"Yep," she said.

All of them grinned at each other. Okey shook his head and went off to bed. The girls headed for the television. And Ellie sat with her mother.

"You think she's *really* crazy, Mama?"

Her mother nodded her head.

"Anybody who won't live here," she said with pursed lips, "has got to be."

❄ Ellie's Valentine

ONE DAY IN FEBRUARY THERE CAME A SNOW INTO THE mountains that was so big even the old ones couldn't remember any storm ever outdoing it.

It began secretly during the night, and when Ellie's mother called them all out of bed the next morning and they got a look outside, the first thing the girls wondered was if school would be called off.

They turned on their radio to listen for news of the county schools. But the radio announcer said that, as far as he knew, all the schools were open. The county superintendent had not called.

Ellie kicked the bottom of the refrigerator. But her sisters squealed with delight.

Okey said, "Well, praise the Lord. I couldn't have stood staying cooped up with six women in this house." Then he went outside to check on Bullet.

Ellie slowly pulled on her clothes. The real reason she didn't want to go to school was not the staying at home. She didn't want to go because it was Valentine's Day, and she couldn't bear it if no boy gave her a special valentine. She had already considered being sick for the day, but the thought of staying around Okey and her mother and their squawking had changed her mind.

She knew why her sisters were so happy to be going to school. They all had boyfriends and they knew something special was waiting for them.

Nothing was waiting for Ellie but disgrace.

The snowplows had been through during the night, so the only real trouble they had walking to the bus stop was getting out of their yard. Huge drifts lay alongside the road, and the trees suffered under heavy sleeves of snow. It was still dark, for the sun hadn't risen yet, but the snow served as some illumination. The girls tramped out to the stop.

Their bus stop was one of the few that had a shelter. Just a wooden building with three walls and no front, but it kept the wind off on bitter mornings.

This morning, though, the snow had been shoved by the plow right up to the shelter and partly into it. About four feet high. Enough to discourage anybody with cold feet and legs from trying to dig through.

"Oh, no!" cried Eunice. She had taken an especially long time to arrange her hair at home. Standing in the road, waiting for the bus in the wet snow and wind, would ruin her, even with the scarf she was wearing.

"My *hair*!" she cried.

The other girls, less concerned than Eunice about hair matters, ignored her.

Eventually more riders showed up. Judy and Joseph White. C. E. and Cathy Connor. Sonny Mills.

The bus was going to be late. They had already figured that out. So they all hopped and jumped and danced and whistled and whooped and crowed and giggled and shivered and moaned in the road. Waiting for County Bus 53.

And just when they were beginning to give up, just when Ellie was starting to take hope that she could avoid this year's Valentine's Day, the wide thick headlights of the bus came over the top of the half-moon hill and everyone (except her) cheered and stamped, then finally climbed on. She was last.

The driver, Mr. Danner, nodded to each of them. He wasn't usually friendly. Just picked them up and dropped them off. Did his job. Sometimes, though, he'd blow the horn a few times and wait in the road a minute if someone was missing from a bus stop. He'd wait to see if the late one would come puffing over the hill. Or if the rider lived next to the road, Mr. Danner would look toward the front window of the house for a sign of whether someone was coming or not.

Some bus drivers didn't bother to honk or to wait. Ellie knew that, so she decided she liked Mr. Danner.

The bus lumbered along the snowy road on its way toward the elementary school to drop off Ellie and the kids through eighth grade before it headed on out to Monroe County High School with the rest. Ellie sat alone. She looked out the window and silently cursed Valentine's Day and boys and school and her sisters and all that made her plain miserable.

The next stop was at Willie Peters' house. All six kids were at that stop, hopping and blowing. At each stop it looked like almost everybody was making it to school, even the ones who had to walk down off the mountains.

When they came to Blue Jay Six Hill, Ellie wished in her heart the bus might not make it. Might just slide all the way down the hill and back the way it had come. But even Blue Jay Six Hill let her down, and they kept going.

Ellie could just see what would happen at school. They'd make some stupid little valentine to give to their parents or Someone Special the way they always did. Then the boys would sneak around and slide their valentines under some girl's desk top. And Ellie would clean out her desk at the end of the day and come up empty-handed.

She decided she'd make a valentine for Bullet. Let him chew it up good when she got home.

The bus began slowing down for a stop. Ellie looked out the window to see who was waiting at this one, then she realized there was no bus stop on this stretch of the road. Everybody else did, too.

"What's going on?"

Mr. Danner let the bus idle a few seconds, then shifted, pulled the emergency brake and shut off the engine. .

The loud heater stopped blowing and the sudden silence scared them all.

"It's a tree!" someone in front shouted.

Ellie jumped up to get a look with everyone else. Sure enough, it was a tree. A big tree, an old tree, a tree too tired to carry all the snow. And it had cracked and fallen across the road, waiting for County Bus 53 to find it.

Hallelujah, Ellie thought.

Mr. Danner climbed off and stood outside, speculating.

Finally he climbed back on.

"Well, kids," he said, "looks like we gotta hike."

"Hike?"

"No other way to get around it. Can't back up on this mountain, that's for sure. And that tree's not going anywhere. We'll have to walk to the Meadors' on up the road."

Everybody started talking, giggling, full of excitement. Except, of course, the high-school girls, like Eunice, whose plans were falling to ruin.

Ellie couldn't believe her luck.

"Okay now, button up. Gloves on, you little ones. You big ones, too, for that matter. Leave your books and lunches on the bus. We'll get 'em later."

Mr. Danner led the way out the door. And all twenty-eight of them followed. The kindergartners circled around the bus driver, holding each other's hands, and the group started walking.

A little boy fell at once. Mr. Danner picked him up and muttered something about slick cowboy boots.

Laughter and talk echoed from them into the woods. Ellie was thrilled. Not only did it look like she was going to avoid humiliation at school—she was actually having a good time. A real adventure in the life of Ellie Farley. Wait until Okey heard about hiking in the dark morning, stranded, hungry (she'd stretch it a little), searching for shelter.

He'd be impressed.

After about ten minutes of walking, though, some of the little ones started asking exactly how far it was to the Meadors'. Even the big ones didn't know for sure if it was just around the next curve, or the next, or the next . . .

Then, after about fifteen minutes of hard walking on that icy road in the snow and wind with no house in sight, the laughter and the talk got thinner. After about twenty minutes, it stopped. And Ellie was breathing hard, her throat was feeling cold deep down inside, and her eyes were watering up.

Someone in the group of kindergartners sobbed. That's all they needed, all the little ones. They started sniffling, one by one, and before anybody was ready for it, they were wailing.

Ellie decided disgrace, shame and humiliation were all better than what the hike was turning into.

Mr. Danner tried to give the small ones hugs and words of encouragement, but there were eight of them and only one of him.

"My feet hurt," one boy cried, tears streaming warm down his cold, red face.

Everyone waited to see what Mr. Danner would do.

"Okay, Bobby," he answered, "If your feet hurt, let me give you a lift."

To Ellie's amazement, he lifted the child onto his shoulders.

"Now, let's try again, kids. Just a little further on." He smiled at them, patted Bobby's legs and went on.

But another little one started crying. And, to everyone's surprise, one of the high-school boys caught up with her and lifted her into his arms.

It made Ellie almost wish she were five years old.

And as they all struggled along, the smaller ones grew so cold and tired that eventually, one by one, they were each picked up by someone larger.

Everyone was silent. Ellie was sad. And so cold. Worst morning of her life.

Those who were carrying the smaller children struggled not to slip and fall, but some fell anyway. And the two would go down together. Some of the small ones could laugh it off and start all over. But others cried.

Still, somehow, amid the falls, and the bruises, the throats sore from the wind, and the throbbing, aching fingers—somehow in spite of all this, they made that last turn and saw the Meador house up ahead.

Shouts went up. Ellie whooped like her daddy. They whistled and jumped up and down and hugged each other.

They had made it.

The planks of the Meador porch echoed with the stamping of tired feet, then the wooden door opened wide. The warmth of a home eased the coldness from each face as the twenty-eight passengers plus one bus driver dragged inside.

"Oh, you poor children!" Mrs. Meador said as she moved to each one, framing their cheeks with her plump hands. "God love your bones!"

She and her husband and her son James, who had long before given up on the bus and trudged back home, helped pull off scarfs and mittens and coats and boots. When he came to Ellie, James seemed shy but pleased to have her in his house.

He had never quite gotten over the thrill of her Christmas cookies.

"Whew!" Ellie said. "Talk about cold!" James took her things to be laid out to dry, and she huddled on the big braided rug in front of the fireplace with everyone else.

Eunice was feeling her damp, straggly hair, a little pout on her face.

"Shoot, Eun," Ellie said. "Don't worry about it. I bet when Keith Evans finds out you didn't make it to school, he'll hike himself all the way to our house."

Eunice just pouted harder, so Ellie ignored her.

The Meadors were giving out cups of sugary warm tea, and as the kids thawed, they got noisier.

Even Ellie began to feel exuberant again. She had escaped Valentine's Day. And she and all the rest had accomplished something brave and wonderful. And, for this morning, she deeply loved Mr. Danner.

James came with a cup of tea for her and one for himself and squeezed in to sit beside her.

"Some valentine, huh?" he commented.

Ellie sputtered and splashed some of the tea on her pants.

"You can say that again!"

"You hungry?" he asked.

"Huh?"

"*Hungry?*"

"Well . . . sure. I guess," she answered.

"Come on then."

She got up and followed him through the living room, up the stairs to the second floor and into a bedroom.

"This your room?" she asked.

"Uh-huh." He started rummaging through a bureau drawer.

The room had pictures of airplanes covering every wall. Ellie had never seen so many pictures of airplanes.

"You like planes?" she asked.

"Uh-huh." He shut the drawer and started digging into another one.

"I've never seen so many planes," she said, walking all around the room and looking at some of them up close.

"Found it!"

She turned to look at James. And in his hand was a wide, flat box that looked like it might hold handkerchiefs.

He walked over to her and opened the lid. Inside were a Christmas bell, painted red and white, and a stocking, painted pink and yellow with blue trim.

Ellie looked at him.

"You saved these two cookies since Christmas?"

James grinned. "Yep."

Ellie shook her head in disbelief.

"Want one?" he asked.

Ellie grinned.

"They're not *rotten*?"

"Heck, no. This room's so cold most of the time, they could probably keep till June."

Ellie chose the stocking. She bit into it. It was good. A little tough, but good.

"Why'd you save them?"

James shrugged his shoulders and looked shyly away.

"Just liked 'em, that's all. Wanted to make them last."

Ellie sat down on the rug with him and finished her cookie. They drank their tea and talked about airplanes and war and dogs and the hike Ellie had just made.

At home later that night, it occurred to Ellie that God couldn't have made a more perfect Valentine's Day.

※ *Spring*

❃ Okey's Song

ELLIE HEARD ABOUT LESTER WOOD FROM HER DADDY.

Lester was a boy Ellie's age who was running for class president. Ellie considered him pretty boring, too nice to be much fun. He had several older brothers and they sometimes came around to see Ellie's sisters. She was pretty sure they were even duller than their younger brother.

What Ellie heard from Okey was that Lester got shot by one of his brothers. And he was dead by the time the ambulance made the long trip out from town.

Okey said Lester and his brother were target

shooting. And Lester had walked right in front when his brother fired. Just wasn't paying him any attention, Okey figured. Just forgot there was a gun about to fire. Sort of like walking in front of somebody in a swing, forgetting he's going to come back in hard and knock you down.

Ellie went to the funeral. First one she'd ever gone to. Lester looked just about the same to her dead as he had looked alive. She was ashamed she had found him boring then and still did. She told herself that if God would change things and bring Lester back to life, she'd vote for Lester for class president. He sure never hurt anybody.

Lester's sisters were all dressed up for the funeral. They weren't much older than Ellie. She noticed they were wearing nylons and high heels. One had on some bright red lipstick and a pair of dangling pearl earrings. Ellie thought the girl looked pretty, like someone going to a party in town. She spent more time looking at Lester's sisters than at anything else during the funeral.

Nobody cried in the church. Ellie had expected a lot of wailing and carrying on, and she'd been worried for fear it would upset her. But everyone was quiet, with just a little sniffling as if they were all at the tail end of bad colds.

And in a few days, talk of young Lester Wood was over.

Something stuck with Ellie, though. And she went to Bullet with it.

Ellie would come home after school and wander down to the doghouse. Bullet, chained up, would be lying on his side in the sun, dreaming of rabbits, Ellie figured.

Ellie would drop down on the dirt and stroke Bullet's stomach. The dog would look at her, grunt, thump his tail, sigh hard and close his eyes again. Ellie stayed with him for a while for comfort.

It was what she needed. Comfort. She couldn't figure it out because she'd never liked Lester Wood that much, so it wasn't her loss that he was dead.

She would whisper now and then to Bullet what was on her mind.

"I sure am glad you're here, Bullet," she would say. "I sure hope you're here a long time. Longer than me."

She'd scratch under his chin.

"Glad we're all here," she'd say. "Everybody."

Bullet would thump his lazy tail.

"Glad we're not dead," Ellie would whisper.

One thing she and Okey did together, the one thing that set her apart from her mother and her sisters, was the target practice. They had given up on any real hunting since the deer. Ellie realized she wouldn't be able to kill anything. But she handled a gun well, so the practice had become important to her.

The Saturday after Lester was buried, Okey set up some cans and bottles on the fence posts and stood outside with Ellie and her gun.

Ellie raised the rifle and shot off a can. Then another one. She missed a bottle. Bullet started barking because he wanted to hunt. And Okey cussed when she missed.

"What are you doing, girl? Aiming at the skinny part on top?"

Ellie shook her head. She took aim again. But she hesitated. She needed more room. More space. She moved off, away from Okey, to aim again.

"Moving around's not gonna help," Okey complained.

Ellie lowered the gun, looked hard at him, then

raised it to aim again. Okey shifted to his other foot.

Ellie lowered the gun again.

"Daddy, you're making me nervous."

Okey raised his eyebrows.

"What am I *doing* to make you nervous?"

"You moved," Ellie answered.

"I didn't. I been standing right here all the time."

"You scooted a little."

"I don't never scoot, girl."

"Well, your body leaned the other way, Daddy."

Okey looked at her with his mouth half open.

"I think you're plumb crazy. Now, are you gonna shoot or not?"

Ellie sighed and turned toward the targets again. She raised her rifle.

"Now stay there, Daddy."

"What's it look like I'm doing?"

Ellie lowered her rifle again.

"Daddy, how far can a bullet travel? I mean, when I miss that bottle, how far does the bullet keep going? I mean, can it go for a mile if it doesn't hit a tree or something?"

Okey looked at her carefully.

"What is it you need to know, Ellie?" he finally asked.

"I need to know what I just asked you."

"Well, I never heard such a fool question. How come you're interested all of a sudden in how far them bullets go?"

Ellie looked down at the ground.

"I don't want to kill nobody, Daddy."

"Shoot, them bottles and cans are about as dead as they'll ever be."

Ellie shook her head.

"I'm afraid, Daddy. Of an accident." She looked over at him. "Afraid I might shoot somebody. Maybe you. Like what happened to Lester."

Okey looked off toward the trees.

"I figure I got more sense than to walk in front of a gun, girl."

"But, Daddy, I don't mean *you* making a mistake. I mean *me*. I mean, I'm just as dumb as Lester was. Why, dumber. He was running for class president. Now, if he can be that smart and that stupid and get shot, Daddy, I figure I can be stupider and shoot somebody."

Ellie's eyes watered.

"I'm scared, Daddy."

Okey kept his gaze on the woods. Both were silent. Ellie prayed he'd understand. That she wouldn't lose him, wouldn't lose what she had with him.

"Well," he finally said, "I reckon you just need a breather. Some time to get over Lester. Time away from the gun."

Ellie fought against the tears.

Okey walked over and took the rifle from her hands.

"You want to help me fix Bullet's roof? Needs some new tar paper."

So Ellie helped him do that. He told some awful jokes. And he sang a song about a blue-eyed daisy, which made Ellie blush, though she wasn't sure why.

No one seemed to really mind the change in things.

❋ *Best Friends*

ELLIE AND CAROLYN OAKS AT SCHOOL DECIDED TO BE best friends. Ellie admired Carolyn because she had long red hair. Carolyn admired Ellie because she was thin. Neither of them wanted to be a sixth-grade cheerleader and neither of them had a boyfriend. And they both liked dogs.

They sold enough old pop bottles to go into town with some money one Saturday. Carolyn's dad drove them and dropped them off in front of G. C. Murphy's. They had one hour to shop and two hours to see a movie; then, he said, he'd be back for them. Carolyn's dad drove a milk truck for a living, so Ellie figured he didn't mind the extra running around. Okey would have told them to walk—both ways.

The first thing Ellie and Carolyn did was head into Murphy's to the picture booth. They giggled and sputtered, trying to squeeze through the skinny doorway at the same time. Then they scrunched up together on the one stool inside and pulled the curtains closed. Anyone standing outside would have just seen their old jeans and sneakers.

Ellie dug into her pocket for the quarter, jabbing an elbow into Carolyn's side and making her howl. Ellie dropped the coin in the slot.

"Okay, here it comes!" yelled Carolyn. "Smile!" She poked her finger into Ellie's ribs and made her scream. Flash.

They were both laughing so hard, tears were coming and their mouths were big as caves. Flash.

"Wait! Wait! Don't laugh!" giggled Ellie, and they both twisted their mouths into frowns as hard as they could, their bodies still quaking with laughter and their eyes wet with the effort to hide it. Flash.

"Okay, let's get up real close and make a face!"

Carolyn gasped, right after the flash. So they leaned forward right into the camera, pushed their noses up like a pig's, stuck out their tongues, pulled down their eyes to show the bloody part beneath the white and held it. Flash.

They burst into giggles again and stepped on each other getting out. Now that people could see them, they tried to compose themselves. But their shoulders shook and their eyes teared and they hid their heads against the side of the booth in hilarious embarrassment.

It took three minutes for the pictures to come out. It seemed ages, though, and they were just about to go look for the store manager when the skinny sheet of photos slid into the box.

They took one look, then screamed with laughter. They hung onto each other, overcome, then ducked back into the booth and pulled the curtain so no one could see them giggling like hyenas as they looked at themselves.

After a few minutes they emerged, dry-eyed, mildly grinning, and headed for the soda fountain.

They ate banana splits and potato chips, bursting into only an occasional giggle, then hit Main Street.

Halfway down toward the movie theater, Ellie spotted some rings in a jeweler's window. The sign read, "Friendship Rings." They went in.

The rings were wide like wedding bands and decorated with fancy swirls. The idea was to get matching rings, swearing friendship and loyalty as best friends.

"You want to, Ellie?" Carolyn asked.

Ellie took a good look at the box of rings.

"Sure, why not?" She didn't want Carolyn to know how much one would mean to her.

"We'll take two!" Carolyn told the jeweler.

The rings were two dollars apiece, so their money was gone except for what they'd saved for the movie. But Ellie slid on her size four and Carolyn slid on her size six and they left the shop feeling forever bound.

The matinee was a horror film called *Creatures of the Dark*, and Ellie and Carolyn got so scared that twice they had to run out to the lobby to wait for the creatures to finish somebody off. They watched the ladies pop popcorn, admired their friendship rings again and read every line of the "Coming Soon" movie posters. Then they went back inside for more.

After the movie, they found Carolyn's dad waiting for them in front of the theater, just as he'd promised. He drove Ellie all the way home. She prayed the house would be silent when they pulled in front, and it was. Mr. Oaks turned around in the driveway, and Carolyn waved out the window until the car disappeared down the mountain road.

That night Ellie looked at the pictures from Murphy's. They'd agreed to take turns keeping the picture sheet, until one day they'd each choose their two favorites and cut the sheet up. But this first night the pictures were with Ellie.

She loved the look of them—all the gray and brown that hid the things about her that weren't pretty. She liked the slick paper and the lingering smell of chemicals.

Ellie stood the picture sheet up on the chest of drawers and threatened to smack her sisters if they touched it.

She decided not to remove her ring at all. Even when she washed. If it turned green and rusty . . . well, that was better than taking the ring off.

Ellie had a best friend. She was happy.

Ellie
Sees a Fit

IT WAS A NORMAL DAY AT SCHOOL AND ELLIE WAS IN the middle of geography when one of the boys had a fit.

Mrs. Richmond, the teacher, was explaining the culture of Brazil when Harvey McPeak in the third row went into a fit. One minute Mrs. Richmond was talking coffee beans and the next minute she had grabbed a ruler and run for Harvey's desk.

"John, get Mr. Woodrum!" she yelled. They all knew it was serious if the principal was being called.

Ellie couldn't see well because she sat in the

back row, but it was plain that Mrs. Richmond was sticking the ruler in Harvey's mouth. Ellie felt sick to her stomach. She knew she was going to throw up, but if she threw up it would only make things worse for poor Mrs. Richmond—so she didn't.

By the time Mr. Woodrum ran into the room with John, Harvey was lying in a dead faint, Mrs. Richmond was crying, three of the girls were crying, everyone was scared and Ellie knew she'd have to throw up. So she ran for the bathroom while Mr. Woodrum put things in order.

When she got back, shaky and pale green, Harvey and Mr. Woodrum were gone, Mrs. Richmond was drinking a glass of water and wiping her eyes with a tissue and the room sounded like a beehive.

Ellie eased herself into her desk. She looked across at Randy Meadows.

"Harvey dead?" she asked.

"Naw," said Randy. "He came to and walked out with Mr. Woodrum. But he could have been dead. Could have swallowed his tongue, if Mrs. Richmond didn't have that ruler."

Ellie's stomach went sour again.

"Could've what?"

"Swallowed his tongue," Randy answered. "I know because my cousin Ed takes fits and everybody says you have to make sure he doesn't swallow his tongue."

"But how . . ." Ellie began.

"Beats me. But I heard a girl over at Daniels Elementary died last year and that was why."

Ellie didn't say anything. She wished Carolyn was with her, but Carolyn was in music.

Mrs. Richmond finally got the class settled and back on the subject of coffee beans. Ellie wasn't listening, though. She didn't listen to anything the rest of geography. She was wondering what brought on fits.

Carolyn was loaded with questions at lunch.

"Well, what was it like, Ellie? I mean, did you *see* him? Was it awful? Were you scared?"

Ellie said she didn't see him, it wasn't awful, she wasn't scared. She didn't want to talk about it so she asked Carolyn about Jim in music and that took care of that.

But she took the story of Harvey McPeak home to Okey.

"Well," he said. "I've heard of them but never seen one. We never had no fits on our side of the family. I can't speak for your mother's."

Ellie was partly relieved. She asked her mother.

"Fits in the family?" her mother repeated. "Well, seems to me your Aunt Bessie had a few in her lifetime. In fact, I believe it kept your Great-uncle Charles on edge to his dying day. But Bessie lived to be almost ninety, so I reckon they knew when one was coming."

"But how would they know, Mama?"

"Shoot, I don't know nothing about them things. Never had to worry with it myself."

Ellie, though, was worried. She wanted to tell somebody what was troubling her, but who, but who? Somebody who would know the answer and wouldn't laugh at her.

She spent most of the night thinking about it. As she lay in bed, her tongue felt too big in her mouth and her stomach still wasn't right.

The next morning Harvey wasn't at school. Ellie wondered if he'd finally died, but Mrs. Richmond said he was resting and would be back in a day or two. That was all she said.

So Ellie didn't get her answer.

Where could she find out? She was too afraid of Mr. Woodrum to talk to him. Who would know?

Finally, in the afternoon, in the middle of the Civil War, she got an idea.

When she got home from school, she pulled the telephone cord as tight as she could and hid herself in the bathroom to make a call. She got the number from the yellow pages.

She listened to the phone ringing.

"Emergency Room," answered a woman's voice.

"Uh . . ." Ellie couldn't start. "Uh . . ."

"Hello?"

"Are you a nurse?" Ellie asked.

"Yes, can I help you?"

"Well, I was wondering . . . if you . . . if you could tell me . . . uh . . . what causes fits."

"Fits?" echoed the nurse. "Do you mean epilepsy? Is someone having a seizure in your home?"

"Yes, ma'am. I mean, no, ma'am. No, ma'am, no one's having one in my home, and yes, ma'am, that's what I mean."

The nurse didn't answer.

Ellie whispered, "I'd appreciate it if you could tell me what causes it."

"Have you had a seizure?" asked the nurse.

"Oh, no! It was a boy at school. I was just wondering . . ."

The nurse was quiet a moment. "Are you afraid you'll have one, too, honey?"

Ellie blushed.

"Yes, ma'am. Sort of."

"Well, dear, I can't tell you for sure you won't ever have one in your lifetime, but most of us never do. It's an illness that has to do with the brain. Do you feel well?"

"Yes, ma'am."

"Do you faint often?"

"No, ma'am."

"Well, dear, I think you are probably in perfect health and have nothing to worry about. Most likely that boy has had his illness since he was small. And because of what happened, he'll be given some medicine to control his seizures."

"Yes, ma'am," answered Ellie. "Uh, I thank you for talking to me. Very much."

"You're quite welcome, dear."

" 'Bye." Ellie softly replaced the receiver. She felt around the inside of her mouth with her tongue. It felt normal. She didn't believe anyone could swallow his tongue anyway, since it was all hooked up in there.

She stood up and looked at herself in the bathroom mirror. She looked all right. She didn't figure rotten teeth qualified her as unhealthy.

She decided she wasn't going to have any fits. And she was glad about it.

When Harvey came back to school, he seemed shy and embarrassed, and Ellie felt sorry for him. None of the kids really talked to him, and nobody mentioned his fit. Mostly they all seemed embarrassed, too.

If she hadn't been so sure she wasn't going to have any fits, Ellie would have kept away from Harvey like the rest of them. And if she hadn't known he'd been given some medicine to stop any more fits from coming, she would have kept her eyes on him like a hawk.

But she knew he was all right. And she was, too.

So she surprised him—and herself—and especially Carolyn—when she invited him to sit with the two of them at lunch. Carolyn wasn't talking, and Harvey was still shy, so Ellie talked the whole time about Bullet.

❄ A Lovely Night

ELLIE HAD TO GO TO CAROLYN'S BIRTHDAY PARTY, and it was there that she got kissed.

Ellie was scared about going. Her mother had sewn up a pretty white dress with a blue sash for her. Okey said it would have to get her through every party for the next seven years. But that's all he said.

On the day of the party the whole house took to making Ellie beautiful. The older girls knew that it would be Ellie's first boy-girl party, and they remembered things Ellie didn't know about. Since Ellie was youngest, they seemed to feel obliged to do all they could for her.

Right after breakfast Eunice made Ellie wash her hair then sit at the kitchen table while Eunice rolled it up with Dippity-Doo. Ellie's hair had never been rolled up before and she worried she might look like her mother's friends when it came down— all puffed out and stupid. Eunice pulled on Ellie's hair too hard and brought tears to her eyes. The Dippity-Doo began to remind her of Vaseline. Then she wondered if the hair would stick like glue to her scalp.

"You better not make me look foolish, Eunice," she warned.

"You look foolish enough already. You don't need no help there," her sister said. "I'm trying to make you look like a *girl*, Ellie."

Ellie made a face. Eunice's idea of looking like a girl was looking like a beautician, and Ellie didn't trust her.

Once her hair was set and covered with a net, Ellie was handed over to Wanda. Wanda brought out a tray of fingernail polishes and spent thirty minutes fixing up the skin around Ellie's nails— which Ellie didn't know ever needed fixing—and putting a coat of three different kinds of polish on them.

"Now sit there and blow at them a while," Wanda instructed.

Ellie blew for a few seconds, then stopped. Her head had started itching and she stuck a finger underneath a roller to get at it.

"No!" Wanda screamed. Ellie jumped, Wanda grabbed her hand, took one look at the wandering finger, then screamed again.

"Ellie, you fool! Look! You smeared all the polish. You even got hair in it!"

Ellie looked at her lumpy nail.

"Does that mean I've got pink hair now?"

Wanda groaned and did the nail all over again. Then *she* blew Ellie's nails dry and even scratched Ellie's head for her when it itched. Wanda was clearly serious about her work.

Linda loaned Ellie her heart locket and Martha gave her a bangle bracelet. Ellie's mother had agreed to let her wear nylons, so the sisters checked and double-checked their panty hose and found the pair in the best shape. But they belonged to Eunice and the material gathered in big folds around Ellie's ankles, so they had to look again through Linda's and Martha's, because those girls were shorter.

The party was set for seven o'clock, and at six

o'clock Ellie was sitting quietly on the edge of her bed, her hair all fat and curly (pressed down with barrettes as far as possible), her nails pink, her neck bearing a locket and her wrist a bangle. The white dress with the blue sash lay beside her.

Ellie's mother put her head in the room. The other girls had already gone off to their Saturday night events, and the house was empty but for the two of them and Okey.

"You're gonna be late, you don't hurry," Ellie's mother warned.

Ellie nodded.

"You need some help?"

Ellie shrugged her shoulders and kept looking at the floor.

Her mother came into the room.

"Well, stand up and let's get that dress on you. Okey's waiting to drive you on over there." She picked up the dress, but Ellie didn't move.

"Well, Ellie, what *is* it?"

Ellie bit her lip, keeping her eyes down, and said, "I'm nervous."

"About what?"

"Oh—just nervous."

"Ellie, there's nothing in the world to be nervous about. All them kids are your friends. Won't be nobody there you don't know. It's time you started going to parties."

She tapped Ellie's head.

"Come on now, put your dress on. Okey'll start spitting if you're late."

Ellie stood up and slipped into the dress her mother held. The sash was tied. She stood in front of the mirror, seeing in it nobody she knew.

"Now, if that don't look mighty pretty," her mother said. "Don't know what you're worried about. You got to grow up sometime, Ellie."

Ellie pulled on Martha's nylons then buckled up her patent leather shoes.

"Mama . . ." She looked at her mother with begging eyes. "Do I have to go?"

Her mother raised one eyebrow and put her hands on her hips.

"If you don't go to this party after I made that dress . . . well, you sure won't be going to *any* parties, girl, while you're living in this house. Now get your tail on out of this room."

Ellie did it. Okey hardly looked at her as they

climbed into his truck. They rode together and didn't talk.

When he pulled in front of Carolyn's house, Okey reminded her to get a ride back with Debbie Meadows's mother. Ellie nodded her head. She looked at Carolyn's brick house, all lit up and scarier than any place she had ever been.

"Well?" Okey said.

Ellie didn't move.

"Go on, girl," he said. "I reckon Carolyn's itchier than you."

Ellie's eyes lit up.

"I bet you're right!" she answered. And she climbed out of the truck and went to rescue Carolyn.

The living room was full of boys and girls sitting stiff on chairs along the walls. A record was playing. Balloons hung everywhere. And Carolyn stood biting her nails by the refreshment table.

It was a mystery to Ellie later how everyone finally started having fun. But they did. They started dancing. They ate cake and potato chips and triangle sandwiches. The boys took off their jackets.

And some of the girls in heels even took their shoes off so they could dance better, and so they wouldn't be a foot taller than every boy in the room.

And many of them played their first game of spin the bottle.

It was Carolyn's older brother, who was helping with the party, who brought out the bottle. There was a lot of blushing and giggling and sweaty hands. But everyone was willing to play. Even Ellie, though she knew she'd allow only a cheek kiss to anyone.

She had gone through three or four cheek kisses when Harold Johnson spun her. Harold had taught Ellie how to swim at the lake the past summer, so she wasn't worried when they went into the other room alone.

But Harold grabbed her and headed for her mouth. Ellie's eyes got big and she pushed him away.

"Wait a minute! Come on!" Harold said.

"No!" Ellie pushed him again.

"Lordy, come on, Ellie." Harold grabbed both her arms so she couldn't push him.

"Harold!"

And he kissed her. Right on the mouth. Maybe for five seconds. He let her go and grinned at her.

"See?"

Ellie was dizzy for the rest of the party. Her insides were floating and she found she couldn't take her eyes off Harold. She hoped they'd play another kissing game, but everyone wanted to dance.

When Ellie got home, her sisters were still out, but her mother was up. Ellie knew not to ask her where Okey was on a Saturday night.

"Well, how was it?" said her mother.

"Okay."

"Your curl all fell out."

Ellie put her hand to her hair. She'd forgotten what she looked like when she left home.

"Well, Mama, I was dancing."

Her mother looked surprised.

"Dancing?" she repeated.

"Uh-huh."

"Well."

Ellie went into the bedroom and closed the door. She didn't want to take off her dress just yet. And she especially didn't want to wash her hands. Because Harold had been wearing some kind of cologne and somehow the smell had got on her hands. She lay back on her bed and covered her nose with them.

She was still dizzy. Her insides were still floating.

Ellie never before had such a lovely night.

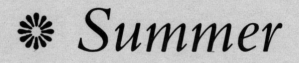 *Summer*

✳ *The Accident*

ONE SATURDAY AFTER LEAVING THE STARDUST TAVERN shortly after midnight, Okey went over a mountain.

They all knew it would happen sooner or later. They knew Okey would drink one glass of whiskey too many and not make it home some night.

But when it finally happened, when the call really came, telling them he was at the county hospital, telling Ellie's mother to get there and quick, they knew they were none of them ready to lose Okey. Ellie most of all.

Okey's red and white pickup lay over the

side of a mountain, smashed and defeated, and Okey lay in a hospital bed in much the same condition.

They called a neighbor and the six of them went to him.

The nurses wouldn't let the girls in to see him. Only Ellie's mother. Ellie waited with her sisters in the glaring light of the waiting room, pacing around the leather couches, reading the names of the candy bars in the vending machine, wishing she smoked so she could have a cigarette or drank so she could have a drink.

Ellie had always thought Okey could never be hurt. He had survived tons of rock falling around him deep in the mines—there should not be anything else he couldn't survive. Everyone worried about Okey driving drunk in his Chevy, even Ellie, but she was the one who was certain he would never die in it. Or because of it.

But when they had pulled in front of the doors of the hospital emergency room, when Ellie had seen the parked ambulances and the white shoes and had smelled the odor that belongs only to a place filled with the sick, she felt she had already lost him. She could not see Okey surviving in such a place.

When Ellie's mother returned to the waiting room after seeing him, she was crying in great heavy sobs that seemed to drag their way up from the very center of her, and they escaped in sounds that made Ellie hurt inside. And she felt more certain she would lose her father.

Eunice and Wanda gathered their mother into their arms and the three of them collapsed on the couch, crying into each other's necks and shoulders and bosoms. Martha slid down onto the floor beside their feet. Linda sat shivering in a nearby chair, with tears running down her cheeks and into the corners of her mouth. And Ellie stood staring at her own reflection in the glass of the vending machine.

Okey was not dead. He was unconscious, his condition was critical, he was fighting for his life, their mother said—but he was not dead.

Ellie stared at herself in the glass and remembered she had not thanked Okey yesterday morning for unscrewing a honey jar for her.

It had been hard for him, with his bad arm, but

he had sat down in a chair, put the jar between his legs to hold it and had used his good strong arm to give it a determined twist.

She had taken it from him and not said thank you.

And now she could not tell him.

"Can't I see him, Mama, please?"

Her mother stuck both her thumbs into the corners of her eyes as if to clog the tears that wanted to flow. She gave a ragged sigh.

"No, Ellie, they said nobody but me. You don't want to see him, Ellie. You don't want to see him." She buried her face against Eunice.

Daddy, don't you die on me, Ellie thought.

Don't you die on me.

She left the vending machine and began pacing again, her fingers twisting in and out of each other, her eyes wide and wet.

And she thought, Must be something I can do. Must be something a girl could do for her daddy who might be dying.

Please Jesus don't let him die.
Our Father don't let him die.
God don't let him die.

None of it sounded good enough. It wouldn't work. She wished she smoked. She wished it was yesterday. She wished . . . and she saw it.

On one of the coffee tables beside a green leather chair. A Bible. Not like her own, since it had somebody named Gideon on the front of it. But it was a Bible.

She dropped into the chair and picked it up. The pages were thin and slick.

Don't die, Daddy.

Using her thumb to flip the pages, she searched. Something good to say to God. That's what she wanted. What you are supposed to say when your daddy might be dying.

A page said: WHERE TO FIND HELP, WHEN.

Ellie slid her finger down the words on the page.

AFRAID. *Yes.*

ANXIOUS. *Yes.*

DEPRESSED. *Don't know.*

DISASTER THREATENS. *Yes.*

FACING A CRISIS. *Yes.*

OVERCOME. *Some.*

SICK OR IN PAIN. *Daddy is.*

SORROWFUL. *Not yet.*

TROUBLE, IN . *Maybe*.

WORRIED. *Yes*.

And she wondered where to turn first, because under AFRAID there were four different chapters she'd have to look at.

But SICK OR IN PAIN made the best sense to her. So while her sisters and her mother huddled together in the middle of the room, Ellie stayed in her chair in the corner and read every verse for someone sick or in pain. She read in Psalms and in Matthew and in Romans and in both Corinthians and in First Peter.

And she didn't understand any of it.

Daddy, don't die.

The night passed. The girls, one by one, fell asleep on the couches in the waiting room. Ellie slept in her chair.

And in the morning, their mother woke them. She told them that Okey was stable.

Did that mean he would die, Ellie asked.

Her mother said no. He wasn't going to die. At least not until he drove that blame fool truck over another mountain.

Ellie cried.

* Old Lady Epperly

OLD LADY EPPERLY LIVED UP TOWARD THE END OF THE road from Ellie's house, so the Farleys didn't see much of her because they were always headed out in the opposite direction.

One day, however, Ellie was taken with the notion to walk on up the road instead of down it. She hadn't any friends living that way, but the sun was warm and there was a chance of finding a full honeysuckle bush.

She puffed up the hill, her feet sliding stupidly on the rocks sometimes, and looked out over the edge, where the Mills family threw their garbage.

The creek ran below and for some reason the Mills family thought it all right to dump their trash outside as long as the creek was nearby.

Ellie liked to look at the dirty, damp boxes and discover what sort of detergent Mrs. Mills used or what kind of cereal her children ate for breakfast. There were more tin cans than boxes, though, and they were boring.

As Ellie came around the turn at the top of the hill, the tall, pointed roof of Old Lady Epperly's house poked into sight. When she came closer, Ellie could see the wide front porch bearing a rocking chair and an old iron pot that held tall red geraniums.

Ellie was just thinking about how much she liked the look of the house and how much she wished her own home had a decent porch when the door opened and out stepped the Old Lady herself.

Ellie jumped when the woman called out to her: "Well, *you've* grown some!"

Ellie walked a little slower and nodded. She sort of smiled. But kept walking.

"How's your *daddy*?" called the woman again.

"Fine." Ellie stopped at the gate beside the road. "He's over to the Farmers' Market in Beckley right now!" She really yelled that last part, since the woman always looked to her the sort of person who wouldn't hear well.

"Which girl are you?" the woman called back.

Ellie knew it was coming. Nobody knew the names of Okey Farley's girls. Just knew them by labels like The Oldest, The Tall One, The Brown-Headed One, The Skinny One, and, in Ellie's case, The One With the Rotten Teeth.

"I'm Ellie!" she yelled back.

The woman nodded vigorously, as though Ellie were just the one of the five girls she'd been waiting for, and she motioned her to come through the gate and onto the porch.

As Ellie was climbing the porch steps, the Old Lady said, "You ever get them teeth fixed?"

Ellie clamped her mouth tight and shook her head.

"Come on in for a strawberry biscuit. I can't get over how you've grown. Gone be as big as your sister—that one, you know, The Tall One, what's her name?"

"Wanda," Ellie answered through her half-open mouth.

"Yes. Wanda." The woman held open the screen door for Ellie. "Too many of you girls to keep up with. Okey should have had a couple of boys. No sane person wants five girls. Shame he didn't have no boys."

Old Lady Epperly's house was warm and dark and full of brown tables with lace doilies on them. The house smelled to Ellie like a quilt just pulled from a trunk.

She followed the woman into the kitchen and sat down at the yellow-painted table. It was the first time she'd been in the Old Lady's house alone. As a guest. The first time she wasn't sitting stiff with her mother carrying on about the new preacher at church or Okey's drinking.

The woman set a jar of preserves and a saucer with two biscuits in front of Ellie. Then she pulled a spoon from a drawer.

"Put up these preserves last summer and nobody to eat them. Here. You try 'em."

The woman slid the saucer and the jar and the spoon closer to Ellie.

"Thank you." Ellie wanted to eat the biscuits, but she was sorry she'd have to open her mouth to do it.

Old Lady Epperly sat down across from her, clutching a dish towel she'd wiped her hands on.

"Well, your daddy still drinking hisself to death?"

Looked like the subject was going to be Teeth or Okey. Ellie was sorry she'd gone up the road instead of down it.

"Some," she answered.

The woman shook her head and sighed.

"Your poor old daddy. Why, Mr. Epperly would have put his life in Okey Farley's hands any day when they was in the mines together."

"*Your* daddy worked with *my* daddy?"

"No, child, my *husband* worked with your daddy. Yes, he'd have done anything for Okey Farley. Said Okey was the best man he knew."

Ellie's mouth was full and she garbled, "He said that?"

"Mm-hmmm. He used to be a good man, your daddy."

Ellie wiped some jam off the corner of her mouth

with her finger. She decided she'd down the other biscuit as quick as she could and be gone.

"You want to see a picture of Mr. Epperly?"

Ellie nodded and stuffed the biscuit into her mouth as the woman waved her into the living room. It was heavy with velvet furniture and the smell of age.

The Old Lady picked up a photograph sitting on top of the television. In it, a man in a uniform held a baby in one arm while the other was wrapped around the waist of a young woman.

"This is Mr. Epperly, here. Ain't he a handsome one in his uniform. He was always a skinny old thing but that uniform fattened him up."

Ellie looked at the woman in the picture.

"Is this you, Miss Epperly?"

"Uh-huh. And that's our first boy—Thomas."

Ellie held the frame in both her hands and stared. The woman in the picture had on a flowered dress with soft, wispy sleeves and a scoop neck that revealed a pearl necklace around her throat.

"Is this really *you*, Miss Epperly?"

"Well, I swan. Sure it's me. Now look there at Thomas's hair. It was pure white like that for years.

Thought he'd get stuck being called Whitey the rest of his life. Give him that fine name Thomas and they stick him with Whitey. But his hair turned pitch-black and that put a stop to it."

Ellie looked at the woman in the picture. And she wished, more than anything, she could look like that woman. Those big shiny teeth. That flowered dress. The smart little hat on her head.

"Miss Epperly, how long did you look like that?"

"You mean *young*, honey?" The old woman held out her hand to take the frame from Ellie and return it to the television.

"No, I mean . . ." and as Ellie looked over to explain, she noticed Old Lady Epperly was wearing a flowered cotton dress under her dark sweater and her apron. And when the woman smiled, she noticed her teeth were still big, but getting rotten like hers.

Then she said, "My daddy always said he liked Mr. Epperly, too."

"I know he did, honey." The old woman smiled and shook her head. "Your daddy was always fond of Mr. Epperly. Okey used to be a good man."

Later Ellie walked back down the road toward home. What she had meant to ask the woman was, "How long were you *pretty*, Miss Epperly?"

How long were you pretty?

When she got back home, she looked at herself in the mirror. Thought about being young. And being pretty. Thought about Okey.

Decided she'd never in her thoughts call the woman Old Lady Epperly again.

And decided when she was old enough, she would get herself a set of big, shiny false teeth and a soft flowered dress.

❋ *Some Year*

BY THE END OF THE SUMMER, MANY THINGS HAD HAP-
pened. Eunice had become engaged to be married
and would be leaving home before Christmas. Bullet had become the best rabbit dog in the county,
so Okey had started loaning him out to hunters—
which meant Okey had more man-talk and was
happier, and sober, more often. He was even thinking about buying a female beagle and raising some
pups. Carolyn had met a boy named Bryan at the
lake and was going with him. And Ellie was waiting for a birthday.

This birthday worried her more than any ever

had. Birthdays had always worried her. In fact, there were two things she never liked: sitting up on New Year's Eve waiting for midnight, and waiting for a birthday. Ellie figured she must be the weirdest girl she knew.

Her mother said she could have a party if she wanted. But she decided not to. Carolyn's party had been the best time she had ever had, and she just didn't want to chance it. She knew in her heart her own would never compare.

So she said no. And asked for a chocolate cake with white icing and for Carolyn to come for dinner with them.

On August 26 then, the pressure cooker was rattling away with a roast inside it, Martha and Wanda were decorating the cake and Okey was going to pick up Carolyn. Ellie couldn't believe it when he offered to, but he did, and Ellie said thank you and meant it.

Maybe it was Okey's brush with death that made this occasion seem important. Maybe it was Eunice's news. Or the summer days that had been so full of time together.

But Ellie sensed that the whole family seemed

really, truly happy about this birthday, her twelfth, whether because they loved her or because they had just been looking for an excuse to decorate a cake and eat it. Ellie's mother started the cooking with no complaint, her sisters didn't bicker, Okey cheerfully went off in the truck for Carolyn and Ellie sat outside with Bullet and wondered at it all.

"Me and you," she whispered in his ear, "had some kind of year, huh, Bullet?"

She thought about poor Lester Wood and Harold's kiss and Harvey's fit.

"Some year," she said, scratching the inside of Bullet's ear.

It was scary to her to turn twelve. Not a teenager yet, but so close she trembled a little to think of it. To think of looking like her sisters in another year.

She kissed Bullet's warm nose and went in to get her gun. She brought it out, set up some cans and started shooting. Okey would be back with Carolyn soon. Not much time left before she'd have to put down the rifle and go on inside. The family would all be waiting.